ST JOHN'S

For Dad   A. MacD.

For Mam   S. F.-D.

Nature note

In nature, beavers – unlike many other animals – do not usually lose their teeth.
They have one set that lasts them all their life. We hope the reader will grant us
poetic licence for Little Beaver's unusual adventure.

First published 2012 by Walker Books Ltd
87 Vauxhall Walk, London SE11 5HJ

2 4 6 8 10 9 7 5 3 1

Text © 2012 Amy MacDonald
Illustrations © 2012 Sarah Fox-Davies

The right of Amy MacDonald and Sarah Fox-Davies
to be identified as author and illustrator respectively of this work has been asserted
by them in accordance with the Copyright, Designs and Patents Act 1988

This book has been typeset in Veronan Light

Printed in China

British Library Cataloguing in Publication Data:
a catalogue record for this book is available from the British Library

ISBN 978-1-4063-2066-4

www.walker.co.uk

Little Beaver
and the
Big Front Tooth

Amy MacDonald

illustrated by Sarah Fox-Davies

WALKER BOOKS
AND SUBSIDIARIES
LONDON · BOSTON · SYDNEY · AUCKLAND

One day Duck and Otter and Turtle went to visit their friend

Little Beaver in his house of mud and sticks.

"Come out and play!" they called.

"Nuhn-unh," said Little Beaver. "Can't."

"What's the matter?" asked Duck. "You sound funny."

"Are you sick?" asked Otter.

"Don't you like us any more?" asked Turtle.

Little Beaver didn't answer.

His friends waited and waited.

But Little Beaver didn't come outside to play.

Finally his friends went away,

looking sad.

When they were gone,

Little Beaver came out of his house.

He was feeling scared.

One of his big front teeth was loose.

It was so loose, it felt like it might fall out,

right then and right there.

How could he be a beaver

if he didn't have

any big front teeth?

Little Beaver looked at his reflection in the pond.

He thought and thought.

At last he had an idea.

Maybe he wasn't a beaver after all.

"Maybe I'm a woodchuck!" he said.

Woodchucks looked like beavers,

without the big front teeth.

Woodchuck's house was in a big field behind the pond.

Little Beaver went to see her.

"Am I a woodchuck?" he asked. He mumbled a little

so she wouldn't see that his tooth was funny.

"No," she said. "Woodchucks live in holes.

You live in a mud house."

He was not a woodchuck.

Little Beaver thought and thought.

At last he had another idea.

"Maybe I'm a muskrat!" he said.

Muskrats lived in mud houses.

Muskrat's house was in a marsh by the river.

Little Beaver went to see him.

"Am I a muskrat?" he asked. He kept his head down
so Muskrat wouldn't see that his tooth was funny.

"No," said Muskrat. "Muskrats eat fish.
You eat bark."

He was not a muskrat.

He was not a woodchuck.

Little Beaver thought and thought.

At last he had another idea.

"Maybe I'm a porcupine!" he said.

Porcupines ate bark.

Porcupine's house was in a tree high up on a mountain.

Little Beaver went to see her.

"Am I a porcupine?" he asked.

Luckily she was too far away to see

that his tooth was funny.

"No," said Porcupine.

"Porcupines live in trees. You—"

"I know," said Little Beaver sadly.

"I live in a mud house."

He was not a woodchuck.

He was not a muskrat.

He was not a porcupine.

What was he?

Little Beaver thought and thought,

but he could not think of the answer.

He decided to go back home.

On his way he passed Wise Old Beaver,

who lived in a mud house

at the very end of the pond.

Wise Old Beaver was chewing bark off a tree

with his big front teeth.

Little Beaver tried to talk

without opening his mouth very wide,

so Wise Old Beaver would not see

that his tooth was funny.

"I'm glad I'm not a porcupine,"
said Little Beaver.
"If I was a porcupine,
I'd live in a tree. And I do not
know how to climb trees."
"Uh-huh,"
said Wise Old Beaver.

"I'm glad I'm not a woodchuck,"
said Little Beaver.
"If I was a woodchuck,
I'd live in a hole. And holes are scary."
"Uh-huh,"
said Wise Old Beaver.

"I'm glad I'm not a muskrat,"
said Little Beaver.
"Muskrats eat fish. And I hate fish."
"Uh-huh,"
said Wise Old Beaver.
"I love bark," said Little Beaver.
Wise Old Beaver said nothing.
"I love to eat bark,"
repeated Little Beaver,
"with my big front teeth."
Wise Old Beaver kept
right on chewing
and saying nothing.

"Could somebody still be a beaver," asked Little Beaver,

"if he didn't have any big front teef?"

He meant to say "teeth", but at that very moment

his loose tooth fell out and the word came out funny.

"Yes, he could still be a beaver," said Wise Old Beaver,

without looking up from what he was doing.

"He might be a very wise old beaver.

When beavers get old, sometimes their teeth fall out."

"Oh," said Little Beaver sadly.

He was pretty sure he wasn't an old beaver.

"Or he might be a very foolish young beaver."

"Really?" asked Little Beaver, sitting up straight.

"Yes. He could be a foolish little beaver
who didn't know that when a tooth falls out,
a new one grows in right away."

"What a foolish little beaver," said Little Beaver.

"Very," said Wise Old Beaver. "But wise and old,
or foolish and young, he is still a beaver."

"Yeth, he ith," said Little Beaver.

"I mean, yeth, I am."

And he went off
to find his friends.